HOW THINGS CAME TO BE

INUIT STORIES OF CREATION

INHABIT
MEDIA

Published in Canada by Inhabit Media Inc.

Nunavut Office
P.O. Box 11125
Iqaluit, Nunavut
X0A 1H0

Ontario Office
191 Eglinton Avenue East, Suite 310
Toronto, Ontario
M4P 1K1

www.inhabitmedia.com

Credits

Edited by Neil Christopher and Louise Flaherty
Written by Rachel and Sean Qitsualik-Tinsley
Cover illustration by Patricia Ann Lewis-MacDougall
"When Things Came to Be," "The Land's Babies," "The Battle of Day and Night," "Feathers and Ice," "The Deep Mother": Illustrated by Patricia Ann Lewis-MacDougall
"Introduction: Grand Sky and the Strength of the Land," "How Caribou Came to Be," "How the Sun and Moon Arose," "The Storm Orphans," "The One Who Is Tied": Illustrated by Emily Fiegenschuh
Cover and interior design by Neil Christopher/Inhabit Media Inc.

978-1-77227-259-8

We acknowledge the support of the Canada Council for the Arts for our publishing program.

This project was made possible in part by the Government of Canada.

Library and Archives Canada Cataloguing in Publication

Title: How things came to be : Inuit stories of creation / written by Rachel and Sean
    Qitsualik-Tinsley ; illustrated by Emily Fiegenschuh, Patricia Ann Lewis-MacDougall.
Other titles: Inuit stories of creation
Names: Qitsualik-Tinsley, Rachel, 1953- author. | Qitsualik-Tinsley, Sean, 1969- author. |
    Fiegenschuh, Emily, illustrator. | Lewis-MacDougall, Patricia Ann, illustrator. | adaptation of
    (work): Qitsualik-Tinsley, Rachel, 1953- Qanuq pinngumirmata.
Description: Reprint. Previously published: Iqaluit, Nunavut: Inhabit Media, 2015. | Adaptation of:
    Qanuq pinngumirmata.
Identifiers: Canadiana 20190136545 | ISBN 9781772272598 (softcover)
Subjects: LCSH: Creation–Folklore. | LCSH: Inuit–Folklore. | LCSH: Tales–Nunavut–Qikiqtaaluk Region.
Classification: LCC PS8633.I88 Q36 2019 | DDC jC813/.6–dc23

HOW THINGS CAME TO BE

INUIT STORIES OF CREATION

Written by
Rachel and Sean Qitsualik-Tinsley

Illustrated by
Emily Fiegenschuh
Patricia Ann Lewis-MacDougall

INHABIT
MEDIA

Contents

Introduction:
Grand Sky and the Strength of the Land

Do we just imagine that things end?

It seems unlikely that one can have a beginning without an end. Inuit imagined an end for this world. But the *world* is such a tiny place. With its problems and struggles, it is sometimes easy to imagine the world ending. As generations passed, Inuit noticed those problems. Their imaginations began to work.

No matter how sad or scary things got, Inuit held out hope. They hoped, because they believed in more than this little world. They knew there was a Big Everything.

As for this little world, it was just the Land. The Land was delicate. Not always stable. Inuit called it *Nuna*. This was the surface world, and Inuit imagined different endings for it. Some thought the Land might crack open. That fire would rise up and engulf everything. Others wondered if the Land had a weak spot, something that a powerful being might kick in order to knock the world out of place.

As for the Big Everything, Inuit called that *Sila*. It was maybe the most important word they knew. It could be used in many ways.

"Weather" was Sila.

"Air" was Sila.

"Sky" was Sila.

"Everything" was Sila.

Sila was all that one could think of. It was all that lay beyond imagination, too. Sila was the Grand Sky. And that's why, when someone was very, very wise, Inuit said that they were "One of Grand Sky."

Inuit never thought of the Grand Sky as having an end. Why would it? Inuit were very practical. Their common sense told them there was no need to say that the Big Everything would disappear. Who might end it? How? And why? They could not imagine any single being calling "Stop!" to Everything. There were many beings on the Land, in the Sea, and in all the worlds under the Grand Sky. There were furred folk. Feathered folk. Tiny beings. Giants. Invisible creatures and living shadows. None, however, were greater than the Grand Sky.

As Inuit shared the world, they did not feel that they were the reason why Everything existed. Did anything exist for a reason?

Inuit tried to be humble, understanding that they were just one part of something infinite. As for whether life was good or bad: that was up to them. It depended on how they treated each other. They did not bother to imagine a Creator who wanted to someday shut down Creation. Life was not a project.

Some Inuit did imagine something like a Creator. But when they did, this was deeply personal. Like loving a favourite song. Mostly, Inuit tried to respect each other. If someone believed something, that was up to them.

Inuit never worshipped. But they loved deeply. They loved the Land around them. The Sea. The Sky. They hunted in order to stay alive. Life came from life. Life fed on life. Life returned to life. Only this mystery was sacred.

Lives could be big, or small. They could have vast powers, or little power at all. But no matter how powerful a being was—even if it was the inventor of day or night—it was still a fellow being. The thinking of those early folk was: Why should one being worship another?

Whether walrus or plant root, Inuit knew that everything in nature wished to hold onto its life. Yet there was no life without eating. Human beings could not survive without hunting or picking the occasional plant. But, since all life held power, every life was worthy of respect.

There was no lasting death, since life force–whether from seaweed or human being–could not be destroyed. How could one destroy power itself? So, Inuit were most concerned with the treatment of other beings. If one were disrespectful to another life power, one deserved that power's anger.

As Inuit saw it, this was the most sensible way to view the world. Did it not require a power, of some kind, to make the Sun shine? To make lightning flash? They believed that the powers of the first beings were greatest of all. So great that they could become whatever they wished.

A person could become the Sun itself, or the Moon. It was will that drove all. Rage, fear, love: these could move the Land and Sea.

Inuit looked around them. They watched the world. They learned about the Grand Sky. They saw how nature behaved, from the tiniest snowflake to the largest storm. And they believed that they, as children of it all, were simply part of its pattern.

That is why life could shift. It could change, but never truly die.

A beginning suggests an end. But an end suggests a beginning. Since Inuit did not conceive of an end to the Sila, they also never thought of a time when the Sila began. The Sila was like life. Life was like the Sila.

And life, like the heart of all, was always there.

All life, they said, was breath.

Inuit called their breath anirniq. Some Inuit knew that the breath only seemed to move in and out of the lungs: in truth, it always returned to the Sky. The Grand Sky comes to the body as a bit of breath. It stays in a body–whether of a person or a seal or a white bear–for a short time. Like a traveller, it moves on.

Life's true home is always the Grand Sky.

If every word up until now has seemed like part of a big bundle of riddles, that's good. Inuit liked riddles. Their Grand Sky people, their wise folk, liked to speak in such riddles.

Inuit put those riddles in their stories. It was how the wise communicated with each other (without being bothered by fools). And it was why Inuit told their stories, over and over, to their children. They understood that, in their own way, children are very wise.

Inuit watched the Land. They understood that little things become the great powers of the world. A snowflake becomes part of a storm. A ripple in the water joins a great tide. A ray of light is the sun's warmth, melting away winter snow.

One who hears a story may remember it, and with memory may come understanding. The child grows with understanding.

The child becomes a new person of Grand Sky.

There are few of Grand Sky left today. The world simply hasn't produced many wise folk, lately. Only now does the world seem to be waking from a long sleep.

Luckily, a few Grand Sky people have kept the stories. They've remembered. This makes them more than wise, perhaps. It means they're guardians. Because of them, other wise folk may come to be.

All the wise were once children. They sat listening to those first tales. Those first songs.

They listened to the deeds. To how the world began. They heard of the Land. Of the great Strength that was its life. They took in the knowledge of how those first beings shaped the world, like a child playing with clay.

In those days, so long ago that time meant nothing, the Land could hear the beings on its surface. Maybe it still listens. But in those old days, the Strength of the Land could be moved by emotion, by will.

In the long ago, humans walked side by side with furred and feathered folk. They spoke to hidden beings, those who kept secrets for the Land. As with all other life, people were Strong. Their Strength, which flowed from the Land and its mysteries, could make whatever they dreamed.

So their dreams were real. Or maybe it was that they shared a dream with the Land itself. What can be called real inside of one great dream?

Some dreamed and came to live deep under the Sea.

Others dreamed and became the Sun or Moon.

Others became Thunder. Lightning.

As things were dreamed, so they became.

These, the Grand Sky folk tell us, were the days of Strength.

1

When Things Came to Be

It was all so long ago. Where was time? It had not yet been dreamed up.

The Grand Sky people say that stone fell from the Sky. Soil, too. All the things of the Land.

Once stone and soil had fallen, babies came. They emerged from the Land like flowers. Life came from the Land. There was little difference between animals and humans. All were equal beings. Every creature could understand every other. They lived with each other. Learned from one another.

They were family.

There was life in those days, but no death. Nor was there light, until someone cried, "Light!"

Nor was there darkness, until someone cried, "Dark!"

The Sky hugged all of existence. Yet it was without a Sun.

There was no Moon.

Today, if a plant springs up, there's a reason for that. If the wind blows, there's some cause behind it.

Yet the sensible things exist only because they're now willed to make sense. In the beginning, will was all that drove creation. What is will but the dream of someone who is awake?

Will was the only force that gave sense to other things. And will was all that animals and humans really owned. The will behind

living things was Strong, in those days. It was Stronger than the Sea. It was as Strong as the Sky.

Those first folk were so Strong that they could do anything. A thought, a wish, a sudden emotion: such things could change the Land.

They lost their powers over time, but every one of those early folk were like powerful shamans. For a while, their powers were like waking dreams. But, as in a dream, they were confused.

People stumbled about in a kind of twilight. They wondered who they were. What they should do. They grew quickly. They found children, new beings like themselves. Life was always rising from the Land. They raised the children. They imagined words to sing to them. They created toys and tools.

They built an entire world from their imagination.

Because they imagined themselves to be hungry, the people grew hungry. They wandered the Land, willing things to be as they went. There was nothing to eat but dirt. So that was what they swallowed.

It was an unpleasant life, because there were no limitations. The people understood growth. But not death. So they became older.

Then older still.

And very weary.

Some folk grew tired of walking. They lay down, refusing to be human anymore. They became hills, their ribs becoming rocky ridges.

One day, someone kicked at some mounds of dirt, and thought about all the stuff that had been created. Those folk who had not become hills had continued to wander. They had become attached to their things, and soon there was too much to carry.

People needed help. This person, kicking at the dirt, let the waking dreams move through him. The Strength of the Land shifted.

The person cried out a new word:

"Dogs!"

Mounds of dirt came to life, blowing sand in every direction. Howls rose on the wind. When the dust settled, there stood newly created dogs. Ready to help, they pulled the first sleds in that dreaming world.

With dogs, humans could move faster. They could spread out in every direction. They began to cover the entire Land.

Yet as they went, time passed.

People began to forget that they were one family with the animals. They came to believe that the animals were separate from themselves. That humans were special. They began to see the animals as little more than living clots of soil. Of dirt.

It was forgotten that the animal folk had risen, alongside humans, from the same Land.

In forgetting, a few humans began to see themselves as better than animals. Less and less did humans and animals enjoy each other's company. They dreamed of their own ways of life, as though they were different nations. They forgot how to speak to one another. And, today, only the very wise remember how to speak in the animal way.

It was not long before humans began to see differences between each other.

People learned how to say things like:

"I am important. And you are not."

"I deserve goodness. And you do not."

"I should have love. And you should not."

They were still powerful, in those days. But power and ignorance together made them dangerous. People continued to dream, and their dreams became real. Less and less did they find children, Strong beings like themselves, on the Land.

They used their Strength to divide themselves. At last, permanently, the people willed themselves to become two sorts of being. As male and female, they hoped to have children of their own.

So those early people dreamed and made families. And the families began to see differences between each other. There was pride. Envy. Anger. And with all those feelings, there came fear. The families spread out, away from each other.

They swelled in number.

Humans were growing more distant from the Land. They no longer ate soil. In order to eat, they hunted the furred and feathered folk. The animal folk did not like this. But they were no wiser than the humans. They had already come to eat each other.

Some wise animals remembered that the humans had been their family, long ago. Life had to feed on life. So the animals agreed that, if they were treated with respect, they would allow themselves to be hunted.

They would allow themselves to die, for a time, until their souls chose a new body. They would die to be reborn into a new form. Like a person changing clothes.

Yet if they were not treated well, the animal folk would withdraw into hidden places. Then, the humans would go hungry.

Under the power of dream, those old days were strange. Though the human beings sometimes went hungry, no one died. None had yet imagined death.

There came a day when a few people grew weary of the Land. They lay down, like their ancestors who had become hills. Their breath simply stopped.

When others found that they had died, they respectfully covered them under piles of stones. But the dead were not yet skilled at dying. Some changed their minds about being dead. They stood up and shrugged off the stones.

No one, in those times of power, knew how to stay dead. Imagination could make them alive, or make them dead. But neither of these states meant anything. So, they dreamed especially forceful dreams.

17

Their wills reached up into the Sky.

After that, when they died, their life force became bright as flame. They burned with colours, like blossoms in spring. They learned, finally, how to leave their bodies behind. Their souls rose up like rainbow fire. They played together in the Sky.

Those people are still there, as the *Aqsarniit*–the northern lights that dance across the night Sky. They'll be there until they will themselves to live somewhere else. For no life can truly die.

So it was, in the Strong days. Since then, it is as though the Land has gone to sleep. The peoples of the world–humans and animal folk–have a new dream. They dream, now, that they have no Strength at all. But that's just as well.

Some Elders say that, in the long ago, the peoples of the Land were too powerful. They imagined storms that scoured the earth. They shook Land and Sea with their tantrums. Their dreams even produced great floods, which is why we find seashells at the very tops of mountains.

It was dreams that filled that early world with wonders. With dangers. Maybe that's why the humans and animals now will themselves to have less Strength. For what is power without wisdom?

For those who doubt, here follow a few deeds of those times. The tantrums. The strangeness. The foolishness.

And the wonder.

2

The Land's Babies

It has been said that, in those earliest days, when folk were Strong, they found babies on the Land. The days of Strong dreaming were very strange. Here's how the Land's babies appeared.

Just as strange powers were shared between animals, people, and the Land, so Inuit and the Land were almost of one mind. In this way, the Land reacted to the good or evil that lay in each soul. No one understood it. No one could say what the Land was thinking (or if it really thought anything at all). But at odd times, it seemed to cast its favour on certain people.

Such favours, those of Grand Sky sometimes say, included the gift of babies. These were human children. They looked the same as any other person. They were Strong, like all beings from that time.

They simply did not emerge from any woman.

These babies were born of the Land itself. Somehow they were fashioned along the secret paths in the Land. The places where the world now hides its Strength from humans.

In those days, the Land's Strength was everywhere. It was not the sort of power that one had to seek out. Nor was it a craft that might be learned. It was part of the wisdom lacing the Big Everything together, at a time when all that is today hidden seemed clear and open.

Yet there was a lot of strangeness, too. It was as though the ways of things had not yet been set.

One such bit of strangeness (and an unwelcome sort) was that of women birthing no children. There was female. Male. But only rarely parents.

The Land itself, then, had to lend these poor women a hand. The Land gave rise to sons and daughters, babies that might be collected like so many eggs.

Maybe the Land created such babies out of pity. Maybe, by word or will or dream, the women themselves coaxed the Land into doing it. One way or another, it was the custom of those strange and ancient folk to search for their babies on the ground.

If a woman wanted a female child, she only had to search about at the edge of camp. There were many baby girls waiting to be found nearby. Males, however, were always found much farther out. Retrieving them was a bit of an annoyance. Males were only for those who didn't mind the trek.

Some unlucky few found no babies. That was very unfortunate. For, in those times, Inuit treasured children of any kind. All babies received the same affection and attention, no matter their origin.

There were still many wise people–Grand Sky folk–around at that time. They knew that real love had nothing to do with the source of one's birth.

As was said, there are not many Grand Sky folk about these days. The few there are speak only rarely about the Land's children. When such babies are spoken of, it's to point out how the original Inuit spread out across the Land so quickly. The Land's children, they say, explain how Inuit became so great in number.

It's not known (or at least not told by people of Grand Sky) how women came to birth children with the frequency that they do today. Nor is it known how or why the Land stopped giving them infants. But, if people today are descended from those powerful folk of long ago, then it's at least comforting to think about one basic fact.

Everyone has one ancestor in common.

The Land itself.

3

The Battle of Day and Night

It has been said that there were times before night and day. Few things moved the Land's Strength more surely than a song. But what if song battled against song? This was how night and day came to be.

There were days, though nearly forgotten, when the Land lay dark and heavy with power. That power was there for all beings to use. It was for good or evil. For beast or human.

There was too much power.

An idle word. An irresponsible thought. A wish. A dream. These could alter the world.

This force ran in the veins of the Fox. His fur was grey and his mind was keen. His great pleasure was to raid the places where Inuit had concealed their food. Such tasty treasures were hidden under rock piles. Though the world was a lightless place, it was no challenge for Fox to sniff things out. Under his blanket of shadow, Fox raided at will.

Life was indeed sweet.

Until the light came on.

One day, Fox was halfway into a pile of rocks when there was a flash out of nowhere. He at first assumed that it was a torch, perhaps some approaching Inuit. He pulled his head from the rock . . .

And was blinded.

Squinting, his eyes at last adjusting, he could see that the entire world had become lit up. He shuddered, feeling naked and exposed.

After his initial confusion came anger. His power rose like waves within him, so that he willed the light away. It obeyed, and went out like a torch tossed into water.

Then it went on again. Fox hissed at the brightness of it.

Tensing, the baffled Fox sent Strength pouring from himself, across the world, smothering the light with his will.

It went on again.

Fox let out a scream of frustration.

"Oh, so you're the one doing that!" called a voice from above.

Fox looked up to see Raven. His feathers were black as soot and he wheeled through the air overhead. Fox hissed again. He knew of the annoying bird. Said to be the most ancient of animal folk, it was rumoured that Raven might have created all others (though the bird himself had not bothered to remember how).

Fox had always questioned the wisdom of such a creature, a bird whose greatest power was to annoy others. Raven's feathers were said to have started out white. The bird had offended someone, who had tossed soot at him. The blackness had been with Raven ever since.

Raven settled on a nearby rock, cocking his head to regard Fox through one pebble-like eye.

"If you say sorry," said Raven, "I'll forgive you. But stop mucking with my light."

Fox stood atop his rock pile, shaking with fury.

"So you're admitting it!" Fox seethed. "You're the one who keeps throwing this ugly glow over everything!"

Raven said, "I'm just trying to touch things up a bit."

"Well, it's not going to continue," spat Fox. "Do you think I want people to catch me stealing their food?"

"So your crimes are my problem?" Raven asked, turning his

head to gauge Fox with the opposite eye. "I like eating, too, you know. And I miss half the things that fall dead around here, because it's so dim. Besides, don't you find it a bit . . . depressing?"

But Fox, by now, was tired of feeling belittled by Raven. He again lashed out with his Strength. Raven's words trailed off into shadow.

The darkness, however, was brief.

Raven piped out his own words of power, his Strength spreading new light across the Land.

And so it went, with bird against beast against bird. Will and words began to flow and intertwine, like currents struggling over the course of a river.

It seemed, after a while, that the Strength was like a whirlpool between them. They battled by song.

Raven chanted:

> "Light-light-light!
> Let-it-be-day!
> Light-light-light!"

Fox chanted:

> "Dark-dark-dark!
> Let-it-be-night!
> Dark-dark-dark!"

At last, the two finally withdrew from each other.

As though by some silent agreement, each animal returned to his lonely ways. Each was exhausted, nearly broken in Strength.

And it is said, in the rumours of those times now beyond any creature's memory, that Raven's will was the greater of the two– though not by much. Through the Strength of his song, he overcame the ancient darkness.

So light was given permanence in the world.

Fox's power has left its mark, though. When light grows weary, and the Strength from Raven wavers, the world falls back into that darkness of old.

Then there is the dark of Winter.

Then comes the long night.

4

How Caribou Came to Be

*As the power days passed, too many wrong things came to be.
They came to be because of carelessness. Heartlessness. Greed.
Ambition. But a few foolish deeds resulted in good things. This was
how the caribou arrived.*

Some events baffle even the folk of Grand Sky. The Land seems to
enjoy its pranks on human beings. A deed comes along, from time to
time, that seems at once wonderful and foolish. And born of a very
simple, ordinary thing.

There was a particular camp.

One day, a strange young man settled in that camp. No one
knew him. They had no idea where he had come from.

He never ate a thing. Nothing at all.

Yet eating nothing, in those times, was not quite as strange as it
is today. To the camp, the important thing was that the stranger was
wealthy. His clothes were odd, but beautiful. He came in on a sled
drawn by many healthy dogs. He had arrived like a sudden blizzard,
and been made welcome.

Soon, the stranger married one of the camp's young women.
There was a great celebration. One more hunter–especially a skilled
one–was always welcome.

Yet days passed, and the stranger never seemed to hunt. His
wife began to complain. She had to beg for food from her relatives.

At first, the situation was scandalous.

After a while, it seemed criminal.

The other hunters of the camp confronted the stranger. They were not gentle. They tried to shame him into providing for his wife.

The young man seemed unmoved at first, until his face finally darkened. Wordless, he seized his great spear. Without a backward glance, he walked out of camp and into the hills.

Some, including the stranger's own wife, had grown to dislike him. A few even hoped that he would not return. Maybe, voices whispered, he was one of the hidden folk–the inhuman folk–whose comings and goings were along unseen paths in the Land.

Maybe camp life would be more peaceful without him.

The young man returned, however. He carried a bizarre animal carcass high on his shoulders. He threw the animal, a light-brown thing with head prongs that looked like gnarled driftwood, at his wife's feet. Pointing to the beast, he spoke a single word, calling it tuktu.

"Caribou."

It was the first time that Inuit eyes had ever beheld a caribou. The wife's hunger overcame her fear. She soon stuffed herself with the peculiar beast. As her belly filled, her complaints faded like windblown smoke.

She ate a lot of caribou after that. The stranger never did become a great hunter. But whenever his wife grew hungry, he hauled in a new tuktu. In time, the wife shared bits of caribou with her relatives. They shared with others. The entire camp knew the animal's taste. The situation was peculiar. Even a bit frightening. Still, the camp folk resigned themselves to the fact that the stranger and his wife ate odd things. And they left them in peace.

All but one, that is.

There was, in that camp, a crafty hunter. He was better than most hunters. He was also familiar with the hidden powers lying rich within the Land. And he had realized that the young stranger could be nothing other than a *tuurngaq*. For lack of a better word, this was a kind of spirit.

The crafty hunter watched the stranger. He sensed that, wherever the stranger went, it must be to a place full of Strength. And bounty. There were many creatures for Inuit to eat, but who knew what was available to a spirit?

Watching the stranger made the crafty hunter feel confined. It made him feel small. Weak. Why could he not have what a spirit had?

So, he followed the spirit-stranger when he next went out among the hills.

The marvels he witnessed!

The hunter followed the spirit-stranger to an isolated spot. It was the sort of plain and trackless ground that spirits were said to prefer. There, he hid and watched as the spirit-stranger raised his spear high.

He then plunged the spear into the earth. Its tip pierced rock as if it were water. And as the spear was withdrawn, out with it came a single caribou. The animal emerged as though born from the Land. Its body flowed out from the Land, following the spear tip until hooves, antlers, and tail were free of the earth.

Neatly, the Land closed behind it.

Panting with excitement, the hunter waited until the spirit-stranger had killed this caribou. The spirit-stranger threw the beast over one shoulder, as if it were lighter than a toy. Then the odd being strode back toward camp.

Once he was sure that the spirit-stranger had left, the hunter sneaked down to the spot where the spear had pierced the Land.

His mind flashed like lightning, imagining how the camp folk would praise him for bringing back animals of his own.

He would have food forever.

He would be admired forever.

Yet there was no sign of an opening. Frustrated, and eager for animals as soon as possible, the hunter gripped his knife. He knelt.

He plunged the blade into the Land, ripping as though the ground were no more than an unwanted pelt.

Out of the earth poured endless caribou–an entire herd of animals. It is said that the hunter was thrown back by their force, and there was nothing that he could do as the creatures battered and knocked him about. He could only scramble for his life.

The beasts were uncountable. They seemed to flow from the living ground, as though they were also spirits of a kind.

They drummed across the earth in the hours that followed, flattening all that would not yield before their hooves. They feared nothing that stood on this strange new landscape, the surface world. Their herds spread across the tundra, like blood from the wounded Land.

When those of Grand Sky speak of this time, they tell that, by the strange knowledge of spirits, the stranger soon learned of what had happened. He knew that the arrival of caribou was a catastrophe.

The caribou herds had come from somewhere beyond the Land. Somewhere beyond understanding. There were none left in their original home.

Every existing caribou had escaped onto the Land.

The spirit-stranger was furious. He knew that there was no way to send the animals back. The animals were fierce, in those days. They were terrible. They trampled everything as they went, threatening creatures of the Land.

So the spirit-stranger used his anger. He used it to call on the Strength of the Land. His power came down on the heads of the caribou. It gave them a furious knock. And this is why a caribou's head is flat to this day.

The effect was that the caribou grew timid. They came to fear other beings. They ran. And they ran. Always, they ran from other life, ranging far across the tundra.

Inuit were now able to hunt the caribou. The animals became one of their most important foods. A source of bone and antler for making tools. The best kind of clothing and blankets for Winter. But the caribou made Inuit work hard in order to catch them. And to the spirit-stranger, still angry at humans for releasing the animals, that was just fine.

Even the folk of Grand Sky have since debated the events of that time. Was this the greatest theft under the Sky? Or its greatest blessing?

Whichever the answer, caribou had arrived on the Land.

5

How the Sun and Moon Arose

It has been told that day and night arose by a battle of wills. But the coming of light didn't mean there was a Sun. Or a Moon. Those arose from will, too. There was no battle, though. Only shame.

In the days of power, when all creatures knew the same language and traded one skin for another with ease, the world was still soft. It was pliable.

There was room for newness, for great good. Evil as well. Living forces carved it like wind and water on ice.

The world was the greatest sculpture of all.

Even in the days when people spread out across the Land, they didn't sweat under any Sun. Nor did they camp beneath a Moon.

There was plenty of light in the Summer days. Dark in the long night of Winter. The earliest powers had already settled on day and night. But these conditions were matters of will. They were part of the Strength of those times. When no one had yet dreamed that things should make sense.

Under the Sky, Inuit played. Hunted. They were becoming more like the people of today. They knew sadness and betrayal, by then. Pride and shame.

Yet they were still Strong folk. They were close to the Land. It listened closely (maybe too closely) to their hearts. The people of that time could change themselves. But more and more often, they did not become what they wished to be.

They became as they felt.

Folk of Grand Sky tell of a brother and sister.

The two were the best of friends. They were close to the same age, old enough that many considered them adults, but young enough as to remain busy at play.

Like all humans by that time, they lived in a camp with others. But they were like a family of two. Whenever problems arose, the brother and sister tackled them together. They had agreed to be the ultimate team. To never work against each other.

For this reason, they were proud. Their chins were held higher than those of any others in camp. Their eyes flashed with Strength. They congratulated themselves and each other for their successes in life.

In those days, just as today, young people had their own friends. Their own interests. They wanted privacy. Times away from those who were not of their own age.

The adults were understanding, then. It was traditional to make a big shelter in which youths could gather. In that shelter, there was constant laughter. The young had their privacy. They could do whatever they wanted. They played games in their shelter.

Playing–that was almost all they did.

Grown-ups would walk by the shelter, hearing the laughter. They would shake their heads, but smile.

The young folk had their favourite games. One was called "lampblack." The light of the shelter was a seal-oil lamp. It would be snuffed out. A random person then sneaked through the darkness, trying to dab soot on the nose of anyone they chose.

It was a silly little game of stealth. The real fun was in laughing at whichever individual wore a black nose when the lamp was once more lit.

The brother-sister pair were maybe the best players of all. They always managed to avoid getting their noses blackened. Somehow they could tell whenever someone was sneaking up on them. However dark it got, they always dodged left, right, maybe backward, before a hand reached out for their noses.

They were as stealthy as they were wary.

Between them, they had dabbed a lot of soot on a lot of noses. They always giggled together, later on, recalling the embarrassed faces of those who had been laughed at—noses black as a bear's.

There came the evening of one particularly large gathering. Every youth came to play in the shelter.

Someone suggested that they play lampblack.

The light went out. All around there was nervous tittering and giggling from the many players. An unknown someone was already on the prowl. That someone had retrieved soot from a pot. And they were . . .

The sister pulled back suddenly, startled. Someone had brushed her face.

Someone had managed to get her nose!

She cried out, already thinking of what she would look like to the others. She tried to console herself. To reason that it had only been a matter of time. Somebody had been bound to put soot on her.

The sister swatted at empty air, hoping to at least touch whoever had brushed her. But that person had already pulled back.

At the sound of her outcry, the shelter filled with excited laughter. She tried to laugh along, despite her embarrassment.

The light eventually returned.

Every gaze in the shelter went to every other—settling on the sister. Still, she forced herself to laugh along. Inside, she burned, hating the experience and wanting to hide. But there was no denying the soot on her nose.

In only a few heartbeats, fingers came to point in the sister's direction. But there was something unusual, frenzied, in the laughter of the group.

The sister was alarmed. Confused. Why were people laughing more than usual? Were the fools so happy to see that it was her face, usually so proud, now blackened with soot?

Not everyone was pointing at her.

The sister's eyes followed some of the other fingers.

Then she saw.

His fingers were black. Her brother's. He, of all people, had put soot on her face.

The forced laughter died in her throat. The sister stared at her brother, sitting with his black fingertips. He wore a crafty smile. He was clearly pleased with himself.

The smile disappeared when the eyes of the siblings met.

Staring, rigid as one trapped in ice, the sister sat. Her cheeks burned hotter than a lamp flame. All around, accusing fingers swept back and forth, from brother to sister to brother. Mocking laughter flooded the sister's ears.

Her brother had made a joke of her.

Her.

The proudest one in camp.

He had made a fool of her.

His gaze became panicked. Apologetic. As though to convey some lie that he had not meant to target her. But then the sister's eyes fell to the floor of the shelter, and she could think of nothing other than betrayal. She could feel nothing other than shame.

They had swom to work together. To be a team.

How could he, of all people, have tumed her into a laughing stock?

She arose.

Maybe it was the look on her face. Maybe they all sensed the wrath that suddenly blazed from her core. Whatever the reason, the laughter of every youth drained away, like water seeping into cracked earth.

Still, their mockery echoed, louder than ever, in her own mind.

Her brother began to plead. He babbled something about jokes. About meaning no harm. His words seemed like the whine of summer mosquitoes.

The sister wiped soot and tears from her face.

She fled.

Disgrace trailed like heat behind her.

Outside, by the door, she sighted a single torch. It was reserved for relighting the lamp after the game. She stood by it for a moment, staring into its flame. The orange and red of it curled like a tongue around her soul.

Strength moved through flame and sister.

Other youths emerged from the shelter. There were gasps, a few screams, as each pair of eyes found the sister.

She was high above them.

She herself looked down, smiling at the way her bare feet dangled over the camp. It seemed as though she had become one with the torch fire. Like a windblown spark, she went Skyward.

The sister clutched the torch in her hand. She held it high, as though to guide her. The Strength surged through the flame and her own being, so that they became one.

She rose fast.

High.

Her humiliation burned hotter than fire. It took her away from the place of shame.

Behind her, she could hear the shouts of her brother. He was crying out. Begging for her return. Demanding it. She caught one last glimpse of him, his upturned face looking pale and pocked in the weak light below.

She turned from him forever.

By her will, she carried herself still higher. She went beyond sight of the camp. To where there was only cloud and the rush of wind.

Then she went higher.

The wise folk say, of that sister, that she remained in the Sky. Her burning heart went out forever over the wide Land. Some like to think that she yet bears the torch that she seized so long ago. That it still lights the way along her endless journey. Maybe it's the torch that burns. Maybe it's her.

Is there any real difference between them now?

She is still called by her name.

Siqiniq.

"Sun."

The brother is still there, too. But his will is less than that of his sister. He, the shameful one, shines with a lesser light. Some like to say that it's because, having no torch of his own, he holds only a few smoldering coals.

His name is *Taqqiq.*

"Moon."

He'll never stop chasing his sister. He's proud. Stubborn. He will not give up on trying to catch her (whether to apologize or force her back to earth, no one can say).

Yet what he wants does not matter, in the end. She's even prouder. In all this time, she has never stopped. Nor even spared him a backward glance.

In this way will the Moon's coldness, until days when the Land is finished, trail behind the Sun's fire.

6

Feathers and Ice

What is a story? Is it tiny? Tidy? The folk of Grand Sky have tales within tales. Stories that wind like Arctic willow roots. They have grown over time, bits added to bits. Now they have to be handled like chips of ice. Treat them with care. They melt away.

Everyone knows that Inuit know ice. And they know it well. In all its states. In all its ways. But their Grand Sky folk say that there was a time when the Sea was free of ice.

There were no icebergs. No cracks spanning all the wide Sea. That ice came later. It was the result of one man.

The man's name was Kiviuq.

Well, he was barely a man. Almost a boy. But if one were to speak of Kiviuq's entire life, the Sun might have circled the Land by the time that telling had finished. And that would be the short version.

Kiviuq's doings, the things he saw, the places he visited, were so many and so bizarre that few can now remember them all. Most people know, however, that Kiviuq was a wanderer. He was said to have paddled from one end of the world to the other in his little Sea qajaq, his one-man boat.

Kiviuq always seemed to be something between a hero and a fool. He was a clever hunter. But he was an even more clever shaman. A shaman was a person for whom the hidden forces in the world never quite stayed hidden. A shaman was someone good at controlling the special powers of the Land and its beings.

Such powers, however, were often the source of Kiviuq's problems.

Like many young men, Kiviuq liked girls. He was on the lookout for a female partner. Unfortunately, he had a tendency to attract monsters. They often started out looking like women, but they usually ended up being an animal in human form. If he was lucky, it was a loon. Or a fox.

Generally, they were much worse.

For a shaman, one who was supposed to see the hidden powers, Kiviuq was kind of bad at recognizing shape-shifters.

So he was delighted when, after all his "marriages" to various creatures, he found an actual human. She lived alone, tending to her drying racks and nice, clean bedding. Kiviuq was wet with Sea water when he paddled up to her rocky shore. He appreciated her offer to shelter him and dry his clothes.

It was not long before she said he'd make a good husband.

Well, she was very nice. She seemed like Kiviuq's ideal partner. It was a bit odd to find a wife simply waiting for him, in a summer tent on some lonely shore. But Kiviuq was just relieved that she was not a mermaid. Or a giant clam. Or a cannibalistic hag.

He settled in with her, becoming quite content.

Until he heard her laugh.

Her laughter was insane–high and wild. Like whistling wind. It chilled his blood. Every time Kiviuq tried to sleep, he was kept awake, terrified by his wife's mad laughing.

In time, he fell asleep. But his dreams were filled with something unseen, a blade or other sharp object that kept poking him.

At some point, his eyes opened.

He realized that he was being attacked. His bed contained sharp pokers. They moved on their own, jabbing him over and over. Kiviuq wasn't a complete idiot. He quickly realized that they were directed by his wife's powers.

She was a shaman. And, like too many of his other wives, she was trying to kill him.

Panicking, Kiviuq called on his own Strength. His powers whipped themselves up into a fierce white bear. The beast went to his wife and roared in her face. It distracted her long enough for Kiviuq to snatch up his clothes.

Trying to run while putting on his parka and boots, Kiviuq stumbled his way to the pebbly shore. He wanted his qajaq.

He risked a glance to his rear and saw her.

His wife had her ulu in hand. It was a great big crescent knife she used to slice up animal hides. Hers was especially large. She let out a howl when his eyes met hers. She raced down to the shore, blade slashing at the open air.

With practised ease, Kiviuq slipped into his qajaq.

Soon, he was far out on the water. He could see her back at the beach, cursing and gesturing with her blade. He let out a sigh of relief.

Yet she was not done with him.

Kiviuq had been right in assuming that the woman was a shaman. What he did not suspect was that she was far more powerful than himself. Maybe he should have known. The folk of Grand Sky, after all, say that some women make Stronger shamans than men (just as children can make Stronger shamans than grown-ups).

Such was this woman's anger, as she stood on the shore, that she was able to pour awful Strength into her ulu. The blade had served her well over the years. In some odd way, it had become a part of her. Now, she growled to it, even sang a bit, using words that few people today remember.

She unleashed a snarl with Strength in it.

Her will swirled in on Kiviuq.

She hurled her blade.

Kiviuq, being a shaman himself, felt her power like a whiplash

across his back. Hunched as much in terror as in effort, he paddled with his breath gasping, his limbs burning. All the while, he wheezed his own little Strong songs, hoping to speed his escape.

He turned at one point, hearing strange noises behind him.

Alone, the ulu was there. Driven by the woman's anger, it skipped and danced across the water.

The blade was alive. It was coming toward Kiviuq.

With every hop, the ulu seemed to cast up Sea spray. Up came walls of foam and water. Each wave was seven times higher than whatever had been sent up behind it. Great plumes of white now obscured the shore.

Worse, the Sea was freezing.

Everywhere the wrath of the woman touched the Sea–everywhere her ulu skipped–ice spread like a giant's stamp on the water.

Still, Kiviuq was aided by his own songs.

Working like never before, he managed to outdistance the dancing ulu. At last, it seemed to tire. He turned in time to see it sink beneath the waves.

Yet the ice remained.

The Sea kept freezing. Solid whiteness even crept ahead of Kiviuq. His little qajaq was nearly trapped in the expanding ice. He struggled to find paths around icebergs that rose like great white blossoms.

He sang and he paddled. He used all of his knowledge.

At last, he slipped away.

Since that time, some part of the woman's will has remained on the Sea. The ice has failed to fully conquer the waters. But it spreads in Winter, like white arms embracing every shore.

As for the spray, it did not fall back to the Sea. It stayed aloft. The Sea spray flared out into feathers. Into wings. In Strength, it came alive. And rose to fly away.

Sea spray, sent up by the woman's ulu, became the first of many waterfowl–those birds who so love the water. All born from the skipping ulu.

In this way, the Land balances terror with beauty.

7

The Deep Mother

*S*ome tales (like which wife chased Kiviuq and why) are not *especially important. The folk of Grand Sky know which stories matter. Their voices go low, serious, when they tell this one. This one is most important.*

The earliest and most powerful of days did not affect only the Land. They also wrenched at the Sea. At the tides. At the beasts within them.

It is said that the lives of human beings came to be shaped by such events. These were powerful doings. Because of such doings, those of Grand Sky understand that deeds, whether good or evil, are not important to the times in which they happen.

They're important to the future they shape.

There is a woman in the Sea. She goes by many names. She's known to many peoples of the Land. Even today. Her will matters: no whale, no walrus, no seal may be caught without it. Without her approval, folk go hungry.

Here is why.

Like all women, she started as a girl. She was not in the Sea, not at first. She lived with her parents. Together, they were a camp of three.

The girl wanted to keep it that way.

She was stubborn. No talk of tradition or acceptability would

move her to accept a husband. It had never been a problem. Until it began to seem that she was refusing every young man who visited her.

Growing up, it had seemed that her parents were her greatest and only friends. She was their only child, the lone mirror of their love. Her days had been spent, at the camps of their little family, in song and laughter.

Yet a change had come.

Her parents had grown strange to her. Now, they never spoke of anything other than a husband. Of leaving. The girl didn't understand why such changes must be. She didn't understand why such things were considered "natural."

So she found venom in her heart. She used it against everyone to whom her parents introduced her. She made sure that there would be no strange men in her life.

With harsh words, she drove every young man away.

A day came when the wind sang across the waves. The Sun flashed. The girl looked up from her chores to see a lone boat approaching. It was paddled by a single youth. This time, her eyes remained on him as he came near. This time, she did not run into hiding.

The girl's parents welcomed the young man. He was soft-spoken. He was fine. The richness of his clothing matched the beauty of his face.

He spoke to the girl with great kindness. He reminded her of the love she'd come to miss from her parents.

She risked opening her heart. Happy days passed.

They married.

Soon, it was time for the girl to leave. To start a new life with her young man. She was happy. But she still cried as she made her way down to his waiting boat.

Her parents tried to reassure her. They pointed out that they would see her in a year or so. They laughed, trying to cheer her up, adding that they might meet a grandchild when they saw her next.

The young couple left.

Husband and wife travelled, with the Sea like a cold, dark broth around them. At times the girl addressed her young man. But he paddled in silence, hood over his face. His warmth had been replaced with an unexplained coldness.

She grew afraid. She stopped talking.

The boat at last arrived on the shores of a windswept island. It was lifeless, but for birds. There seemed to be a million of them. They watched and wheeled in the air overhead. Their droppings coated every part of the island, making it stink whenever the wind died down.

Silent as ever, the young man grasped the girl by her wrist. With terrifying strength, he pulled her from the boat. She stumbled across sharp stones on the shore.

The young man raised his opposite hand toward his boat. Strength poured from the gesture. The boat sank like a mound of sand under the surf. The girl's eyes widened with fear. She had not suspected her husband of owning such power.

Keeping hold of her wrist, the young man dragged her up from the shore. He brought her to the centre of the island. There, she saw a gigantic heap of trash. Bones. Tattered hides. Driftwood stained with bird droppings.

After a moment, she realized that the heap was an ugly little hut.

Her husband explained that it was her new home.

He laughed at her horrified expression. As he laughed, his voice lost its human sound. It became alternately squawking and trilling. The girl stepped back as she heard it, and her husband released her wrist.

He removed his hood.

Still, he laughed. While he did so, his skin boiled like grease on hot stones.

She screamed as he stepped closer.

By the time he caught her wrist again, his face had taken on a new shape. Its true shape. He wore dirty feathers instead of hair. There was a beak where a mouth and nose should have been.

He shook himself, and she saw lice crawling between his feathers. He regarded her with eyes like pebbles. His beak opened wide. A worm of a tongue waggled at her. He shocked her ears with a great squawk.

The girl stared at her husband's body. It was the same as ever. But his head was now that of a gull-like bird. A Sea bird.

The girl wrenched herself away from his grip. She emptied her lungs in a trailing scream. Finally, she understood that her "husband" was a kind of spirit. A fulmar-spirit. She gulped in another breath. Screamed again.

The fulmar-spirit caught her. It threw her into the filthy hut.

More than a year passed on the island. The girl, enslaved to the spirit, experienced horrors that the folk of Grand Sky speak of only to those with very strong minds. And stomachs.

When a boat at last drew up to the shores of that island, the girl barely recognized the figure it carried.

It was her father.

He and the girl's mother had grown concerned when the seasons had passed without word. He'd finally taken to searching for his daughter. Most people had power in those days, though many were losing it. His Strength had gone out, searching Land and Sea.

And he'd found her.

Yet the girl cut his greetings short, warning her father of the fulmar-spirit. The monster was momentarily absent. It walked terrible paths along the world's edges, where it met with other horrible beings of the Land. Whenever it did so, it left her under the watchful eyes of the island's birds.

The father's face paled as the girl explained the true nature of her husband. But he tried to find courage. He swore, then, that he would take his daughter away from this place.

So the girl left with her father. Paddling fast, with his daughter as cargo, the father made his way back across the strange, dark waters.

They had not travelled long when a sudden shriek went up behind them. Father and daughter turned to see a long shadow. It rose high over the island. At its heart lay a birdlike form. The spirit had returned. And it no longer bothered with the illusion of humanity.

It came on, flowing through the air like a living storm.

The father's paddling grew frantic. Clumsy. He mumbled out songs of Strength to lend them speed.

When the spirit next shrieked, the sound was from overhead.

It was already upon them.

The power of a song crackled on the father's lips. The girl sensed something of her father's Strength rise up. It stung the spirit like a great bee. She watched as the spirit cried out, dipping with the pain of the attack. She could feel its own power reaching out, wrestling with her father's Strength.

Still, the father sang.

Still, he paddled.

His words became halting.

His strokes grew strained.

The monster twisted like a vast, black rag in the wind. The girl sensed it gathering itself up.

She felt her father's power shatter.

She was numb. In her horror, she clutched at the tiny boat. She was sure that the spirit would destroy them both. But then she felt hands on her, and before she could so much as turn . . .

She was thrown overboard.

The cold of the water was shocking. It denied her lungs the ability to scream. She could only gasp.

Still, she kept a grip on the side of the boat. She held it with both hands. Her teeth were bared like those of a dog.

She clung with all her stubbornness. All the will she'd ever possessed.

She looked up to see her father. He had tossed her overboard. He was trying to sacrifice her to the spirit. To let himself get away. She saw his expression: sadness mixed with fear.

The girl opened her mouth to beg his assistance. But her words faded when she saw what he held in his hand.

His knife.

She knew what he was thinking, then. He'd decided that he had made a mistake. He'd decided that he should never have tried to rescue his daughter. He was about to remedy his error.

The girl managed a half-cry as the knife touched her fingertips.

Yet she held.

The folk of Grand Sky say that this was the worst of all crimes–a parent harming his child. Such betrayals wound the world. And those folk trying to live in it. They leave it with deep scars.

The Grand Sky folk say that power moved. The world kept her finger joints–those pieces of her hands cut away by her own father.

Power moved, and some pieces became the first seals.

Power moved, and other pieces became walruses.

Power moved, and still more became the whales.

So the pieces of the girl's hands did not die. Neither did the girl.

Instead, she sank.

And sank.

As she sank, the Strength of the Sea flowed through her. Her hair streamed out like ocean currents. Her tears mingled with brine.

And she changed.

No one can now tell of the will or way by which those original powers bonded with lives. The world does seem sleepy, when it was once more active than a child at play. All that's known is that, back in that day, Strength reached out to the girl.

One might imagine that, instead of crying, she laughed at its touch. For she would never weep again.

Only roar.

And will herself down to the Sea's bottom.

Here was her true home. Her adulthood. She was a new and permanent power in the world. Descending fishlike, her hair flowed outward, each strand seeming to touch on some part of her watery domain, until she settled at its very centre.

From the Sea's heart, she ruled.

She was then *Kanna* ("This One Below").

She was *Samani* ("Out at Sea").

And *Sanna* ("Down There").

On every coast and in every part of the Land, she had a different name. Yet Inuit would most often name her *Nuliajuk*. Ever after, *they* would pay for the weakness of Nuliajuk's father.

She's no longer the slave of any spirit. Instead, the spirits come to her. To serve. With them as her spies, she searches for the weaknesses of human beings. Ready and eager to punish, she searches for humanity's dark side.

She no longer has any faith in goodness. She has become a being of pure wrath–like the Sea when it rages.

And if she grows too disgusted with how people treat each other, she withdraws their food.

To the Sea mammals, the whales and seals and others, she is a kind of mother. How could she not be? Those animals were born, after all, from her fingers. And if she wishes to hide them, so that people can no longer hunt, there's little that anyone can do about it.

Yet they can do a *little*.

In the worst of times, there are shamans who can send their souls out and down into the deep. There, they may fight their way past the spirit horde guarding the Deep Mother. If they can reach her, a simple gesture might calm her enough to release the Sea mammals.

She cannot hold a comb.

So, the shamans comb her hair. And they talk to her. They promise to guide folks. To get them to treat each other better. So she isn't so reminded of how she herself was treated. And they soothe her.

For it seems that, while her heart remains broken, there's still some part of it belonging to a girl.

It has not yet forgotten love.

8

The Storm Orphans

*T*he Strength of the Land pulsed and flowed, making new things. But wisdom was already fleeing from the world. There were monsters in Land and Sea. Lurking horrors. Yet there was no monster greater than human cruelty. Here is what cruelty made.

The first folk were wise in the days of power. No thought or wish or dream of living creatures went unnoticed by the Land. But this was never meant to last. Weakness was already creeping into the world. Evil spread as human beings became many in number.

The folk of Grand Sky often tell of this evil. What else are they to do, in order to learn from the old times? Wisdom has no meaning unless one recognizes ignorance.

Here is a strange fact: foolish people enjoy each other's company.

So there came a time when an entire camp of fools gathered on the Land. No one can now say what they called themselves. But they might easily be known as the people of Weak Sky. In particular, these fools were cruel. And as cruel folk do when they arise in the world, they caused suffering throughout their time.

Then their time ended.

But it began with what came most naturally for the Weak Sky folk. Cruelty.

In that camp, so long ago, they brought suffering to two young orphans. They were starving, those little orphans. But for each other, they were friendless.

The twins, brother and sister, scraped and scavenged to survive in that cruel camp. They had no living relatives anywhere in the world. The dogs ate more than they did. As the Weak Sky folk saw things, dogs at least served a purpose. They pulled sleds. Guarded the camp.

What could orphans do?

It was not that the Weak Sky folk were trying to commit evil. They simply reasoned that evil came from directly harming another. If they let the twins starve, that was simply "the Land" at work.

Actually, the Land was at work. But in a much different way.

The orphans were often forced to steal. They became good at it. Each acted as a lookout for the other. They were used to the risk. To occasional captures. Even beatings. They'd learned to care for each other.

When one was beaten, the other would act as nurse, tending to bruises and scratches. And, while doing so, each would sing little songs to the other. In this way, their hearts were eased while their bodies healed.

They rarely spoke of their songs. They simply sang them. Both, however, found it odd that they knew exactly the same tunes. Neither had any memory of having been taught. They liked to think that the songs had been the last gift of their parents–smiling people who had died long ago.

Lean times, in that camp, were deadly times for the twins.

Days arrived when there were food shortages. The dogs whined with hunger. Barest scraps were hard to find.

Lack always makes people vicious. And it brought out greater cruelty in the Weak Sky folk. The orphans were barely tolerated in camp. Often, as a grown-up passed by, a boot would come flying out in a kick at one of the twins (sending them both scrambling).

The twins knew how these times went. Soon the kicks would become thrown rocks.

Some families were already eating dogs. All were especially vigilant of their food stocks throughout this time–a fact that made thieving almost impossible.

The orphans spent their nights holding each other, trying to stay warm by the doorways of snow houses. One would try to keep the other quiet as they wept with hunger. The twins always seemed to be waiting. That was their life. Waiting for an opportunity. For a bit of shelter. For a mouthful.

Their moment had arrived, they believed, on a day when almost all of the camp's men left on a hunt. They went from home to home, trying to snatch up anything edible that had been left unattended. But women had remained at camp. And there were large, nasty youths.

There were too many eyes left in camp.

This time, they were both caught.

The beatings were worse than usual.

Bruised, weary from bellies that had been empty for too long, they crawled to a heap of bones and other garbage. There, they spent some time consoling each other, but without real hope.

No matter how much time they let pass, they never seemed to feel better.

Exhausted, they collapsed amid the garbage. They smiled at one another, though they understood that they were dying. Words were unnecessary, as is often the case with twins. Each understood the other's silent thoughts: that death might finally allow them to walk in those other Lands they'd heard of. They believed that, somewhere, there were worlds of plenty. Places where their parents might return to them.

Now, lying among the bones of dogs, the scraps of fur and spoiled hide, they waited.

An unknown amount of time passed. Wind howled over them. Their fading breaths returned to the Sky. Their heartbeats became one with the deep places of the Land.

They began to entertain each other with the songs they knew.

And it seemed, for a while, that even the Grand Sky held still around them. Listening.

When they ran out of songs, they began to play a bit.

Past split and chapped lips, each laughed that being anything in the world would have been preferable to themselves. So they made up a game. In this new game, they took turns suggesting things they might rather have been.

Anything but an orphan.

Maybe because they were twins, they began to pair up the things of which they spoke. Words seemed to blow in with the wind, settling on their tongues. They whispered words for almost everything in the world.

Flame and warmth.

Water and rain.

Flower and leaf.

Stone and lichen.

Wind and snow.

Light and Sun.

Dark and Moon . . . .

Then, with the last of his strength, the boy sat up. He reached for a dry skin and beat his fist against it, sending a boom across the Land. He cried out.

"Kalliq!"

He didn't understand the word that he had spoken. No one had ever heard it before. But it would come to mean,

"Thunder!"

Then, with the last of her own strength, the sister sat up. She locked eyes with her brother. She had found two old flints that someone had tossed aside. She raised these in front of her face, and her brother smiled.

She struck the flints together. And her eyes flashed in the spark. She cried out with her own new word.

"Qaumajaaq!"

She didn't understand the word that she had spoken. No one had ever heard it before. But it would come to mean,

"Lightning!"

The children did not realize that they'd ceased to play a simple game. The words that they had sung to one another belonged to the Land's secret mind. They had Strength. And it was one with the power that had shaped the Land since soil and rock had fallen from the Sky.

In this Strength, they arose. Their bodies sizzled with ancient power. The power lashed out, twin storms, scattering all that was close to them.

The boy's heart thrummed. Like a drum as large as the world. It was Thunder itself.

The girl's eyes flashed. They were sparking flints. With every blink, she wore trails of Lightning instead of eyelashes. She turned her head upward, letting long streaks of Lightning snarl out into the Sky.

Like shadowed halos, windblown hair danced about their heads. They grinned at one another. They touched hands and giggled at the crackle. Neither of them felt heat. Nor cold.

As one, the twins drew in a great breath. This was a special breath. A Grand piece of the Sky.

Then they erupted from camp, ascending in fury, and delight. They rode the winds high. There, they laughed like giants among valleys made of breeze. Hills made of cloud.

They chased one another over all the wide Land. She flashed white across the Sky, storming in and out of sight. He called with a voice that seemed to shatter the air.

Hand in hand, they drew shivers from the mountaintops.

They cast silver and blue across the tundra.

They stormed over the waters.

Their play was glorious. And passing days meant little to them.

Until they suddenly remembered.

And stopped.

Smiles came to them as, together, they halted. They regarded each other. Each knew that the other had remembered the camp, and how the folk of Weak Sky had treated them.

By the time the twins again found the camp, the folk of Weak Sky were busy feasting. The men had stalked and taken many caribou. Laughter and song rang through the place. Many struggled to find room for one more mouthful of meat. Even the dogs lay about with their bellies stuffed. They were like great, mangy bags.

The twins hovered in the distant hills, rumbling.

They looked over that camp.

Then, descending as no storm that will ever again visit this Land, Thunder and Lightning came home.

Among the generations that followed, folk of Grand Sky taught their children's children to respect those twins. They are evidence that the littlest of things, in the Strong way of this world, set the course for greatest change.

Yet how can one forget these twins?

They still exist, ranging as far as they please. Across Land and Sea. They'll never again settle on the ground. They've grown wise. They know, now, that there is no encampment—no place of humankind—that was ever meant for them.

They now ride the Sky and its turnings. They'll fear nothing ever again (though they delight in scaring others from time to time). Thunder and Lightning began together. Thunder and Lightning will always be together. Were they ever given a chance to love anyone else?

As for that camp of long ago, with its Weak Sky folk, they were seen again. It is whispered that the camp was found sometime after the last visit of the twins. Those hunters who happened across it were shaken. They moved on quickly.

There was no longer any life in that once-cruel place. There were only huge, black cinders. Shaped like people. Like dogs.

When they were touched, they fell to dust.

9

The One Who Is Tied

Now comes the making of the End. As with all things, the End is a dream. It's dreamed because a beginning was dreamed before it. It took a long time for the earliest folk to understand the power of their dreams. Even longer to recognize their arrogance.

They walked side by side with the hidden ones. The giants, too. The living shadows. The tiny folk. The clans of beast and bird.

By dream and will, humans sculpted the Land. They came to know, in time, that they were Strong. That the Land was listening. There was power. And it was theirs to enjoy.

That, say the Grand Sky folk, was when people became most dangerous.

There was a son and his father.

One was human. One was not.

The father was a giant. His son was a human, whom he had adopted as a boy.

The father was not the largest of giants. He could use hills like someone might use stepping stones in a stream. He could cross rivers with a hop. But that was minimal giant work.

Mostly, he and his human son survived by cunning. The giant carried his son as he went (some say in his ear, others in his boot). They liked to wander. They enjoyed each other's company. As they went, hunters could sometimes hear their laughter. It thundered over the rocky hills.

There came a day, say Grand Sky folk, when this odd little family grew hungry. So the father and son started looking for good lakes–those that held fish of a decent size.

After a tiring search, they at last found such a lake. But it had a problem.

There was already a fisherman there–a giant.

This was no ordinary giant, either. He filled both father and son with dread. He was like a mountain that could move. By comparison, he made the father look small.

The father giant hunched low among some of the higher hills, hoping that the fisherman wouldn't see him. Both father and son noticed that he'd already caught many fish (though they seemed too small to give this giant a decent meal).

They talked for a while, then finally agreed to approach the giant. They were desperate for some food. When they asked the fisherman if he would share some of his catch–or at least let them try their own luck–he let out a laugh.

When they did not laugh in return, the greater giant snarled. Then he threatened them.

They retreated.

Yet they did not give up.

Together, the father and son came up with a plan.

When the monstrous fisherman next looked up, it was to regard the tiny son. He stood on a hilltop, hurling colourful insults.

As expected, the giant attacked.

As soon as the fisherman strode into the hills, however, the father giant emerged from where he had hidden himself. He had crouched very low behind the highest hill he could find.

With a roar, he threw himself at the far greater giant.

The giants grappled.

Their struggle shattered hillsides. In solid rock, they ploughed deep furrows with their heels. The noise of their struggle was like that of an avalanche. Their gasps boomed. Echoed. Sometimes, they struck at one another–using fists the size of boulders.

The father giant would have fallen if not for his son. As per their plan, the son waited. He watched the battle from a safe distance. He stood patiently, until the giants at last turned around.

Then he was behind the fisherman. The son gathered up every whit of Strength he had. He did not want to let his father down.

He struck.

The son struck at the back of the fisherman's ankle. It was a powerful blow, by any standard. The fisherman's cry was such that it rocked the Sky.

The great giant was instantly crippled. He teetered. The father came around. He caught the fisherman's neck in massive, strangling arms.

Then it was over.

Tales of killings, especially from those days, are too common. They are never feats to admire. But they can at least be lessons in foolishness.

The folk of Grand Sky have something special to say about this murder. For, of all the things that came to be in the days of power, this murder actually caused an End. However odd that seems, this killing laid the groundwork for the world's End.

It set events in motion.

Here's how.

The great fisherman's dying cry went out among the hills. It was heard by his wife. This was a female giant, not quite as large as her husband. She came too late to assist her mate. She arrived only to meet her own end–again, at the hands of father and son.

Two murders, then, spawned all that tumbled after.

The father and son, it is said, eventually found the child of the giants they had killed. It was a great male infant. He was truly monstrous in size. One day, the father and son supposed, he would grow much larger than his parents.

The child's cries shook air and ears. The father and son had no interest in raising the giant baby. So, in order to create a bit of mischief, they wrapped him tightly.

Then they placed the infant near a human camp.

At this point in the story, the father and son fade from telling and memory (as some say they deserve).

As for the baby, he is far from forgotten.

The folk of the human camp had narrow minds. Twisted hearts. They were folk of Weak Sky, people who had become far too common by that time.

They were cruel, of course. And they did not welcome the giant child who had been brought to them. Nor could the infant, bound as he was, make even the simplest attempt to crawl away.

So the people of that camp tormented the child. They used him for sport. They poked. Prodded. Whipped. Harassed. They were small, and so they enjoyed picking on something greater than themselves. They knew that this child would be a huge giant one day, and that frightened them. But they could take that fear and express it as cruelty.

So, as they felt better and better, the baby felt worse.

There came a day, however, when the camp went to play their horrible games with the infant.

But he had disappeared.

They stood confused, staring at the trackless snow. The infant had been bound. No one could imagine where he'd gone.

The folk of that camp had forgotten how the Land binds its power to deep need, raw emotion. The heart is the seat of Strength. And of all emotions (other than love), suffering sinks deepest into the Land.

Some said that it was the baby's howls. Others insisted that he had spent too much time under the open Sky, under the raging wind.

No one knows how the infant merged with the winds. But he did go up into the Sky. There, the child became much more than any simple giant. He became a spirit unlike any that had been seen before.

He was the living fury of storm winds.

People knew the spirit-infant when he howled down on them. When he blinded them with snow. When gusts raked at their skin and eyes. When cold air dried the lungs.

They knew he was up there.

In this way did the child become the *Silaup Inua*: the air's own terrible heart. Later generations hunched and trembled under his scouring storms. They feared the infant's voice.

There were still powerful folk in those days. Some grew concerned over this spirit. A few feared that he had become the very mind of the Sila. Was the Grand Sky now like the Deep Mother? Had the Big Everything finally turned against humans?

Yet the folk of Grand Sky, as existed in that time, knew better. They could tell that some new spirit had housed itself in the winds. They knew little about the being. But they respected his power.

So people let the spirit-infant be.

Most people, anyway.

One day, the Silaup Inua, the spirit that had once been a giant's child, was visited by a powerful shaman. The shamans of that time were weaker than their ancestors. The world had become so many things that becoming had made them unimaginative. As they dreamed of less Strength, so they owned less of it.

Still, this shaman may have been the greatest of his time. He could take flight with ease. He had travelled to other worlds. To see the Moon. More than once, his soul had made its way into the Sea's depths. He had fought countless spirits down there. Combed the Deep Mother's hair.

Now, he wanted to confront the Silaup Inua.

The shaman flew up to find him. Feeling no cold, he hovered among the clouds, searching with the shaman's Strong sight. This sight could pierce the hidden. It could see the unseen.

He smiled, seeing that the Silaup Inua was still a child. Though he was a spirit now, not a real giant, the shaman saw the child as he looked down on the Land. He was impressed with his size. But the spirit-infant was wrapped tightly in furs. And these were bound with many cords.

The shaman laughed. This was a spirit. A monster. But mostly, he was a baby.

Why had so many wise folk feared him?

It is said that when the spirit at last seemed to sense him, the shaman called out. He challenged the spirit to a fight. Strength against Strength. Power against power.

Yet the air's terrible heart made no reply.

So the shaman sent his powers shuddering out from him. He burned like a star in Strength. His display was fearsome. Rainbow fire filled the air.

After he finally withdrew his power, the shaman laughed at the spirit-infant, who had not so much as moved throughout his display. Then he demanded that the infant show his own Strength.

There is no way to know whether or not the spirit-infant understood the shaman. Or knew whether he was in a fight at all.

What is known: the spirit responded.

Sort of.

Inside of his restraints, the spirit-infant twitched. It wriggled one leg a bit. It gave the lightest of baby kicks.

Suddenly, the shaman cried out. There was strange Strength in the kick. Its power somehow moved through his body, like waves lapping at a shore. It struck his mind. His soul. Everything of which he was made.

It also struck the air.

The clouds.

The Land.

The Sea.

And every life in the world.

It made the world shudder.

Because he was nearest, his mind fixed on the infant, the shaman was caught up in a waking nightmare. His limp body began to drop out of the Sky. The shaman was not aware of the fall.

He was trapped in his mind. In a vision.

A vision of the End.

In his mind, the shaman watched the child. He had grown. He was close to breaking his bonds. The child was so huge that the shaman could barely see all of his body. He seemed to take up the entire world.

The shaman watched as the bonds broke. The child kicked again. Not with the light baby kick that had knocked at Land, Sea, and Sky.

This was a true kick.

He watched as the child's foot struck a kind of stone. A stone made of purest Strength. It was the great keystone: the base upon which the world had been founded.

The Land broke open.

It was filled with oil.

With fire.

The fire ignited the oil.

The Land, stone, and all upon it began to burn.

The vision ended in time for the shaman to avoid slamming into the ground. But he wept as he pulled up. He flew far away, still weeping. He feared the Sky ever after.

He was shattered by the knowledge that he had witnessed the infant's final kick. A kick from the spirit unbound.

The Land's future End.

After this time, those of power decided that this spirit had to remain bound. They taught themselves, in later generations, how to ascend into the Sky. This was so that they might lessen the storms across the Land. And they used their own Strength, their own knowledge, to slightly loosen the spirit's bonds.

Enough to keep him comfortable.

But never to release him.

And in those times, they pitied him. They remembered his origins. And they named him *Narssuk*.

"The One Who Is Tied."

About Endings

Do we just imagine that things end?

It seems unlikely that one can have an ending without a beginning. Inuit imagined a beginning for this world. But the *world* is such a tiny place. It's easy to imagine the world bundled (like Narssuk) together with beginning and end. Inuit imaginations worked hard. But the folk of Grand Sky always understood that imagination sets the foundation for things to be. It doesn't promise that anything *must* come to be.

The world might be sleepy. But this doesn't mean that it no longer dreams. If the tales have anything to say, it's that there is no way of knowing what other things will be.

Dreams can be ugly. They can present feuds. Greed. Fear. Betrayal. Darkness that could make one want to never dream at all.

Yet, here is the world. Land. Sea. Sky. It swells with beauty. There are hearts that never forget to love. There are friendships that have never been broken. Families do nurture each other. There is play. Peace. Light.

And wonder.

Inuit endured even their darkest dreams. It was so that they knew what they wanted from life.

The wise folk know that if they fail to dream (whether of dark or light), they risk loss.

What would they lose?

Understanding of the world.

For it is still being made.

Glossary of Inuktitut Terms

Here is a part for those to whom words matter. Parents or teachers will probably find it most interesting. But young folk (those who make the most powerful shamans, remember) who wish to have a look are, of course, quite welcome.

animiq	Literally means "breath."
Aqsarniit	The northern lights.
Inuit	Translates as "persons" or "inhabitants."
Kalliq	Literally means "thunder."
Kanna	Literally means "This One Below." One of the many names of Nuliajuk.
Kiviuq	The main character in a chain of Inuit stories.
Narssuk	An old word, the literal meaning of which is probably "One Who Is Tied/Lashed."
Nuliajuk	One of the most powerful beings of the Inuit imagination.
Nuna	This term means "land," often referred to as "the Land."

qajaq	This is the original word from which the English word "kayak" was taken.
Qaumajaaq	Literally means "lightning."
Samani	Literally means "Out at Sea." One of the many names of Nuliajuk.
Sanna	Literally means "Down There." One of the many names of Nuliajuk.
Sila	This term means "sky," often referred to as "the Sky."
Silaup Inua	Literally means "The Humanness of the Sky." A term used to refer to Narssuk.
Siqiniq	Literally means "Sun."
Taqqiq	Literally means "Moon."
tuktu	The Inuktitut word for caribou.
tuumgaq	Magical creatures, often (but not always) invisible, that can originate from any source.
ulu	An Inuit woman's traditional crescent-shaped knife.

Contributors

Rachel and Sean Qitsualik-Tinsley write fiction and educational works that celebrate the secretive world of Arctic cosmology and shamanism. Of Inuit-Cree ancestry, Rachel was born in a tent at the northernmost tip of Baffin Island. Raised as a boy, she learned Inuit survival lore from her father. Eventually, she survived residential school. Rachel specializes in archaic dialects and balances personal shamanic experience with a university education. She has published over four hundred articles on culture and language, been shortlisted for several awards, and has enjoyed many years as a judge for Historica's Indigenous Arts & Stories competition. In 2012, she was awarded the Queen Elizabeth II Diamond Jubilee Medal for contributions to Canadian culture. Sean Qitsualik-Tinsley is of Scottish-Mohawk descent and learned a love of nature and stories from his father. He originally trained as an illustrator, but eventually discovered greater aptitude with words, his sci-fi work winning second place in the California-based Writers of the Future contest. Rachel and Sean sweepingly met at the Banff Centre, Alberta, spending subsequent decades as Arctic researchers and consultants. Together, they have published about a dozen books as English originals, along with many shorter works. They are inspired by the "imaginal intelligence" of pre-colonial, Arctic traditions (ancient Inuit and the now-extinct Tuniit). Many such works are found in K-12 schools and universities across Canada and abroad. Their young adult novel of historical fiction, *Skraelings*, won second prize in the Governor General's Literary Awards of 2014 and first prize for the Burt Award of 2015.

From a young age Emily Fiegenschuh has been bringing fantasy worlds to life with her pencil. A graduate of Ringling College of Art and Design, her art has appeared in the *New York Times* bestsellers *A Practical Guide to Dragons* and *A Practical Guide to Monsters*, and has been featured in the fantastic art annuals *Spectrum 9* and *Spectrum 19*. Emily is the author and illustrator of *The Explorer's Guide to Drawing Fantasy Creatures*, a how-to-draw book for creature enthusiasts of all ages. Emily lives in Edmonds, Washington, with her husband, several guinea pigs, and two rambunctious rabbits.

Born and raised in the Niagara Peninsula, Patricia Ann Lewis-MacDougall's childhood days were spent in the woodsy setting of Ontario's Bruce Trail. After graduating high school, Patricia Ann enrolled at Sheridan College to study animation in the 1980s and later illustration. She worked for several years as a storyboard artist for Nelvana. She has illustrated several books for children.

INHABIT
M E D I A

Iqaluit · Toronto